The Bremen Town
Musicians

The Bremen Town Musicians

A Tale by Jacob and Wilhelm Grimm
Illustrated by Hans Fischer

Translated by Anthea Bell

North-South Books

New York · London

A man once owned a donkey who had carried sacks to the mill for many years, never tiring. But now the donkey's strength was failing, and he was of less and less use for work, so his master planned to get rid of him. Realizing that something was up, the donkey ran away and set out for Bremen, where he thought he could become a musician in the town band.

When he had been walking for some time, he met a dog lying in the road, panting as if he had been running until he was worn out. "What are you panting like that for, Grabber?" asked the donkey.

"Oh," said the dog, "my master planned to kill me because I'm old and getting weaker day by day. I can't hunt anymore, so I ran away. But how am I going to earn a living now?"

"I tell you what," said the donkey. "I'm going to Bremen to join the town band. You could come with me and be a musician too. I'll beat the drums and you can blow the bugle." The dog liked the idea, so they went on their way.

It wasn't long before they met a cat on the road, looking as glum as three days of wet weather. "Well, old Whiskers, what's the matter with you?" asked the donkey.

"It's no joking matter to have people after your blood," said the cat. "Now that I'm getting on in years, my teeth are blunt and I'd rather sit behind the stove and doze than chase mice. My mistress planned to drown me, but I managed to escape. And now I'm at my wits' end. Where am I to go?"

"Come to Bremen with us. You're good at singing serenades, so you can be a town musician too!"

The cat thought that was a good idea, and went along with them.

Soon the three runaways passed a farmyard where a rooster was sitting on the gate, crowing his heart out.

"Your crowing could wake the dead," said the donkey. "What's it all about?"

"I was forecasting good weather," said the rooster. "Tomorrow is Sunday and they're having guests at the farm. Unfortunately, my cruel mistress has told the cook she wants to make soup of me, so I'm crowing at the top of my voice while I still can."

"I know what, Redhead," said the donkey. "Come with us instead. We're on our way to Bremen, and what we find there will surely be better than death. You can play the clarinet, and if we all make music together it will sound very fine!"

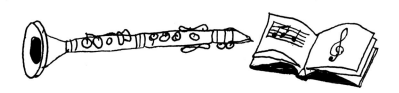

The rooster liked the idea, and so they all four went on their way together. They couldn't get to the town of Bremen in a single day, however, and in the evening they came to a forest where they decided to spend the night.

The donkey and the dog lay down under a big tree, the cat and the rooster got into its branches, and the rooster flew to the very top of the tree, which was the safest place for him.

Before settling down to sleep, the rooster looked around to all four points of the compass, and he thought he saw a little spark of light in the distance. Calling to his companions, he said that there must be a house not so very far away, since he saw a light shining.

"Then we'd better look for it," said the donkey. "It's not very comfortable here."

And the dog thought a few bones with a little meat on them would go down nicely.

So they set off towards the light, and soon they saw it shining more brightly. It became bigger and bigger, and in the end they came to a robbers' house, all brightly lit. The donkey, being the largest of them, went up to the window and looked in.

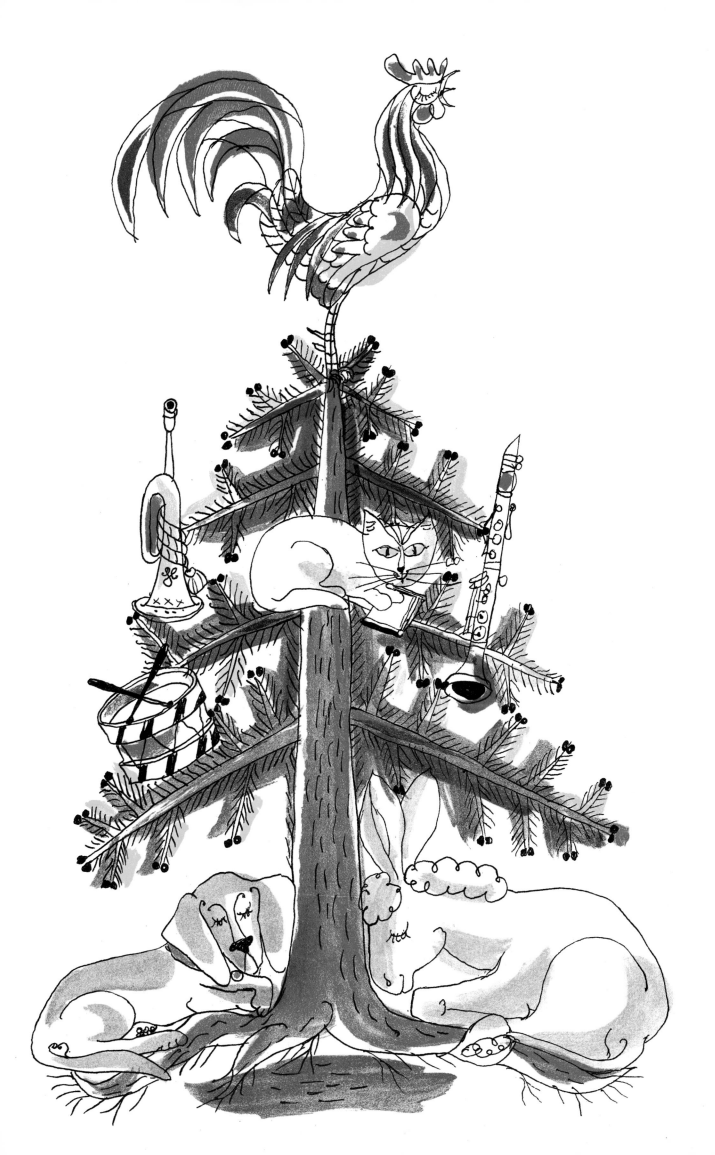

"What do you see, Greypelt?" asked the rooster.

"What do I see?" said the donkey. "I see a table laid with good food and drink, and some robbers sitting at it enjoying themselves."

"Oh, how nice!" said the rooster.

"Dear me, yes, I wish we were in there!" said the donkey.

The animals wondered how they could drive the robbers out of the house, and finally they thought of a way. The donkey propped his front feet on the sill. The dog jumped on his back. Then the cat climbed on top of the dog, and the rooster flew up onto the cat's head.

When they were all in position, one of them gave the word and they began making music. The donkey brayed, the dog barked, the cat hissed, and the rooster crowed. Then they burst into the room through the window, with a great clatter of broken glass.

The robbers leaped to their feet at the fearful noise, thinking it must be a ghost coming in, and they fled into the forest in terror. So the four companions sat down at the robbers' table, and ate as if they weren't likely to eat again for many weeks.

When they had finished their meal, they put out the light and look

a place to sleep, each according to his nature and his own ideas of comfort.

The donkey lay down on the dungheap, the dog lay behind the door, the cat lay on the hearth beside the warm ashes, and the rooster settled on the very top beam of the roof. Being tired from their long journey, they soon fell asleep.

When it was past midnight, the robbers saw from a distance that the lights in the house were out and all seemed quiet. The robber captain said, "We oughtn't to have taken fright like that." And he told one of his men to go and search the house.

The robber crept into the kitchen to light a candle, and thinking the cat's glowing, fiery eyes were live coals, he put the wick to them, expecting it to catch fire.

Well, the cat didn't care for that a bit, and jumped at the robber's face, spitting and scratching. The terrified robber tried to escape through the back door, but the dog, still lying there, jumped up and bit his shin. And as he stumbled past the dungheap in the yard the donkey gave him a hefty kick with his back leg. Then the rooster, roused from his sleep by all the noise, flew past the robber's ear and crowed, "Cock-a-doodle-do!"

The robber ran back to his captain as fast as he could go. "There's a terrible witch in the house!" he yelled. "She spat at me and scratched my face with her long fingers. And there's a man with a knife at the door, who stabbed me in the shin. And there's a huge monster in the yard who beat me with a wooden cudgel. And up in the rafters sits the judge crying, 'Catch that crook, will you?' So then I ran for my life."

After that the robbers never dared go back to the house again. But the four town musicians of Bremen liked the place so much that they stayed there for good.

And the mouth of the last man to tell this tale is still warm.

Hans Fischer, who was known by his trademark signature, *fis*, was one of the most popular Swiss illustrators in the years following World War II, and an important influence in the field of children's book illustration throughout the world.

He was born in Berne, Switzerland, in 1909 and attended the School of Fine and Industrial Arts in Geneva, the School of Art and Commerce in Zurich, and the Fernand Léger Academy in Paris, France. He worked as an illustrator, an advertising artist and graphic designer, and a stage designer and set painter for the legendary Cabaret Cornichon in Zurich. He was well known as a muralist, and his bright, animated works still decorate the walls of public buildings all over Switzerland. He died in 1958.

Hans Fischer also illustrated numerous picture books for children. The first of these, *The Bremen Town Musicians*, was what Fischer called "a household tale," a beloved good-night story that he shared with his children. He would bellow "hee-haw, hee-haw" for the abused donkey, and complained "miao-miao" for the cat. "The louder I crowed, miaowed, hee-hawed, and barked, the more enthusiastic my children became. For the famous attack on the robbers' house, when all the animals stood on each other and screamed in unison, the entire family had to participate with all the different noises. After frequent repetition of the story, and the careful portrayals of the animals, the forest, the night, the robbers' house, and the robbers, it became mandatory for me to illustrate it."

Fischer was fascinated by the way the animals were presented in the Grimm fairy tale—so cleanly, one after the other—and he tried to reflect this in his illustrations by establishing a very strict division of space. Each unhappy animal is introduced on a righthand page and meets up with the growing crowd on the following lefthand page. Since Fischer was used to working with theatrical sets, he eliminated preconceived perceptions about space and the animals' position in it. From the beginning, he places them over each other, as a sort of preview of their famous pyramid scene at the robber's house. Aside from the acrobatic act, this scene becomes a continuous theme throughout the illustrations. Even in the happy-ending scene, all the figures are stacked on top of each other.

In 1944, when the book was first published, this type of minimalism was quite remarkable, especially compared to traditional fairy-tale illustrations. Equally noteworthy were the touches of realism Fischer incorporated into his pictures, showing, for example, how much more difficult it was for the rooster to walk to Bremen than the other animals.

The Bremen Town Musicians, which was first published in Switzerland in 1944, is a fine example of Hans Fischer's mastery of stone lithography, a printmaking process more commonly used for fine art than for illustration. To create the book, Fischer drew the pictures directly onto large stones—one for each color. This same technique was used for Fischer's other picture books, including his interpretation of Perrault's *Puss in Boots* and a story he wrote and illustrated, *Pitschi*, both recently reissued in English by North-South Books.

More importantly, these picture books epitomize the insouciant charm and singular artistry that characterize all of Hans Fischer's work. "They contain everything to delight young people," wrote Bettina Hurlimann in *Three Centuries of Children's Books in Europe*. "They are full of the wit and kindliness, the color and happiness, the great good humor of a man who turned into a child again among his own children."

Hans ten Doornkaat

First North-South Books edition published in 1998.
Copyright © 1944 by Nord-Süd Verlag AG, Gossau Zürich, Switzerland.
First published in Switzerland under the title *Die Bremer Stadtmusikanten*.
English translation copyright © 1998 by North-South Books.

Published in the United States, Great Britain, Canada,
Australia, and New Zealand in 1998 by North-South Books,
an imprint of Nord-Süd Verlag AG, Gossau Zürich, Switzerland.

Library of Congress Cataloging-in-Publication Data is available.
A CIP catalogue record for this book is available from The British Library.
ISBN 1-55858-893-0 (TRADE BINDING)
1 3 5 7 9 TB 10 8 6 4 2
ISBN 1-55858-894-9 (LIBRARY BINDING)
1 3 5 7 9 LB 10 8 6 4 2
Printed in Belgium

For more information about our books, and the authors and artists
who create them, visit our web site: http://www.northsouth.com